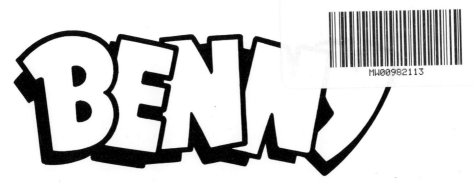

# BENNY

## The Story of a Dog

Diane Wilmer

Pictures by Nicola Smee

**Collins**

For Tamsin and Gabriel,
Benny's first friends.

With thanks to John Grieves,
Veterinary Surgeon, for his
care and advice.

William Collins Sons & Co Ltd
London · Glasgow · Sydney · Auckland
Toronto · Johannesburg

First published 1985
© this anthology William Collins Sons & Co Ltd 1985
©text Diane Wilmer 1985
©illustrations Nicola Smee 1985
©character "Benny" Yorkshire Television Ltd 1984

ISBN 0 00 184090 8

Printed and bound in Portugal by Printer Portuguesa.

# Contents

# Benny comes to the Common

Bella and Jack had always wanted a dog of their own but, for one reason or another, their parents had never got round to getting one for them.

"Wait until you're a bit older," said Dad.

"Yes," agreed Mum. "Then you'll be big enough to look after it yourself."

"But we're big enough now!" insisted the children.

"We'll see," said Mum and Dad, but nothing was ever done about it. Then, quite by accident, Benny came along.

He lived on a barge with a hard, cruel man. They travelled up and down the canals of England and it should have been a good life, full of fun and adventure, but it wasn't. It was awful!

Benny was tied up like a prisoner, he was half-starved and often beaten. He dreamt of running away but it was impossible. Occasionally his master let him walk along the river bank but he towered over him wherever he went and kicked him if he strayed too far from the boat.

Benny had never known love or kindness or the warmth and happiness of a home and family.

Then one bright Spring morning the bargee moored up by Midsummer Common. As soon as he'd left for town, Benny crept out of his corner and peered over the edge of the boat. The air was sharp and clear and birds sang and chirruped in every leafy tree.

"Now, this looks a good place," thought Benny.

"I wonder if there's anyone here to play with?"

Suddenly he spotted two children playing on the other side of the river. They called out to each other as they whizzed a ball back and forth and their happy laughter floated across the Common towards him.

"Hey!" he yelped. "Come over here and play with me!"

The children stopped playing and stared at the scruffy dog, straining at his rope and barking loudly.

"Poor old thing, he looks lonely," said Jack.

"Come on," said Bella, "let's go and cheer him up."

They ran over the bridge and along the river bank to the barge. They didn't dare climb onto the boat but they leant over the side and cuddled Benny.

"Let's be friends," said Jack.

"Oh, yes please!" yapped Benny. "I've never had a friend before."

They were having such a good time that nobody noticed the bargee striding back along the river bank.

"Eh!" he bawled. "What're you doing here?"

The children jumped off the side of the boat and Benny scampered into the nearest corner.

"Oh, don't let him hit me," he whined. "Please don't let him hit me!"

Bella looked at the man and said, "We're not doing any harm."

"We just wanted to see your dog," spluttered Jack.

The man jumped onto the boat and yanked hard at Benny's rope. Benny yelped in pain and tried to cower away in the corner but the bargee dragged him out and shook him hard.

"What' d'yer want to see him for?"

"He just looked very lonely," said Bella, shaking with fear.

"He's supposed to be lonely, you little fool!" snarled the man. "He's a guard dog, not a blooming pet!"

The children watched Benny shivering and shaking on the end of the rope terrified of what the man would do next.

"Now get out of it!" bellowed the bargee. "Before I give

the pair of you a thump round the ear-hole!"

The children turned around and fled with Benny's cries ringing in their ears. He watched them disappear out of sight and felt terrible.

"They've gone, they've gone,
  they won't come back.
  It's the last I've seen of Bella and Jack.
  My wicked master scared them away,
  how can I stand another day,
  on this old barge, with him in charge?
  They've gone, they've gone,
  they won't come back.
  It's the last I've seen of Bella and Jack."

But he was wrong!

The next day the children came creeping back and hid in the bushes until the bargee had gone out. This time they did climb onto the boat and they gave Benny cheese, chocolates and cuddles, but all too soon it was time to go.

"Don't leave me again," howled Benny. "Take me with you this time."

"Can't we keep him?" asked Jack.

"No!" said Bella, very firmly. "That would be stealing. He belongs to the bargee, not us."

"Don't cry," said Jack, giving Benny a big hug. "We'll be back tomorrow."

But the next day Benny had gone!

"We've got to find him!" said Bella.

They raced along the river bank and suddenly spotted the barge heading for the lock.

"BENNY! BENNY!" they yelled and ran faster than ever to catch up with him.

Benny was slumped in a corner feeling desperately unhappy. When he heard the children's voices he sprang to his feet and pushed his head over the side of the boat. The children saw him and stretched out their arms to him.

"Don't go," they begged. "Please don't leave us."

Benny looked at their dear, sweet faces and made the biggest decision of his life.

"I WON'T GO!" he growled, and he started to tug and twist at the rope, wriggling his body this way and that. Suddenly the rope snapped!

With a leap he was up on the side of the boat staring down at the swirling water below him.

"This is it!" thought Benny as he closed his eyes and leapt into the river. SPLASH! It was deep and cold, but Benny

swam for his life. Suddenly the bargee turned round.

"Eh!" he yelled. "Come back here!"

"No fear," gasped Benny. "I'm never coming back to you!"

The man stormed and raged, but there was nothing he could do. Benny had reached the bank and the lock gates were opening wide, the barge was going through.

"Keep the rotten dog!" he bawled at the children. "I'm better off without him!"

He shook his fist at Benny, then grabbed the tiller and set off down-river.

"He's gone," whimpered Benny and began to shake with relief.

"You're ours now," said Bella.

"And nobody will ever take you away again," said Jack.

They ran home across the Common and stopped outside a tall, thin house.

"This is where we live," said Bella.

"Come in!" said Jack.

Benny had never been in a house before and he couldn't believe his eyes. It was big, light and airy, with soft chairs and warm carpets.

The children took Benny to meet Mum and Dad in the kitchen. They were surprised to see such a scruffy, wet dog but when Bella told them what had happened to him, Mr and Mrs Moss felt really sorry for him.

"So, can we keep him forever and ever?" asked Jack.

"You certainly can," said Dad.

"He deserves a good home after what he's been through," said Mum.

"Oh thank you!" yapped Benny. "Thank you very much."

He ran all round the house, sniffing in corners and poking his head in every room. He explored the garden then watched Mum make tea in the big, warm kitchen.

He couldn't believe his eyes when she gave him his own bowl brimming with juicy meat and crunchy biscuits. Dad and the children went out and came back with a big basket.

"This is for you," said Dad and Benny began to think he was dreaming.

That night, when everybody had gone to bed and the house was still and quiet, Benny lay in his new basket and sighed deeply.

"I've come home," he thought happily.

"Home, to Bella and Jack, on Midsummer Common."

**Benny's house**

# Choosing your dog

Have you always wanted a dog of your own? And when you ask if you can have one, do grown-ups keep suggesting you should wait until you're old enough to take care of it yourself?

Bella's best friend, Charlotte, began to wonder if she would *ever* be old enough to have a dog of her own. Then, on her eighth birthday, her parents said she could!

Charlotte was so excited that she wanted to rush out and buy the first dog she saw, but her parents insisted that she thought carefully about it first. Choosing a dog is a bit like choosing a best friend. You're going to spend a lot of time together, so be sensible, and work out what's best for you and your family.

First you must consider the size of your house and the space available, both inside and out. A whopping Great Dane just won't be happy in a one-bedroomed flat and a toy poodle might get lost in a mansion! Charlotte has Midsummer Common right outside her front door so she was able to choose a big dog like Harry, knowing full well he would get all the exercise he needed.

Charlotte discovered that buying Harry was quite an expensive business. The amount you pay for your dog varies a great deal, but you must also take into account his upkeep, the Vet's bills, and his annual dog licence.

Charlotte was lucky. She bought Harry from a breeder and that meant she could see him with his mother, and his brothers and sisters. This isn't always possible. Try looking round your local pet shop, or ask at the animal shelter; they often have puppies in need of a good home.

Wherever you get your puppy, don't be sentimental when you finally do choose. A timid pup hiding in the corner may turn into a nervous, snappy dog. A boisterous pup, demanding too much attention, may become noisy and aggressive. Go for the steady, bright-eyed, clean-nosed, curious pup and *never* buy one under eight weeks old.

Harry's first bed was a cardboard box, lined with newspaper; Charlotte bought him a basket later. She kept him warm and fed him regularly, but mostly she let him settle down, in peace and quiet, to his new way of life.

After a few days, Charlotte took Harry to the Vet. He checked his health and advised on Harry's general condition. Charlotte was pleased. She'd picked a strong, healthy pup and little did she know at the time that he would grow up to be Benny's best friend!

# Benny and the dustbins

Benny woke up one morning to find the house quiet and still.

"Where are you all?" he yapped, but nobody replied.

Dad had left for work, the children were at school and Mum had popped out to the shops.

"Never mind," thought Benny. "I'll soon find something to do."

And, of course, he did!

Bella had left the back door open for him so he wandered out into the garden and saw Charlotte, Bella's best friend who lived next door, feeding her rabbit.

"Hello," she called. "I thought you'd be out playing with Harry."

"That's a good idea," thought Benny and set off to find him, but Harry was nowhere around so Benny sat under the trees and watched the world go by.

> Boats on the river,
> cars on the road,
> pantechnican lorries
> with great big loads.
> Ladies on bikes,
> laughing and talking,
> babies and mums,
> just out walking.

Benny loved it all but by lunchtime he was feeling very hungry.

"I'll go down to the river and pinch some of the duck's bread," he thought but he never got there. He bumped into Harry outside the riverside restaurant.

"Where've you been?" asked Benny.

"Looking for you," growled Harry.

"I'm starving hungry!" whined Benny. "I can't play till I've eaten something."

"Oh, you and your stomach!" groaned Harry. "It's like a bottomless pit."

"It's not my fault if I have a healthy appetite!" snapped Benny. "Now, where can I get something to eat?"

"Right here," said Harry and he nodded towards the restaurant.

Benny gaped at the big, posh pub with its pretty flowers and sparkling paintwork.

"You must be joking," he said. "I can't go in there, I haven't got any money for a start."

"Who needs money," answered Harry with a smirk. "Just follow me."

With his tail held high, Harry snootily led Benny round the back of the restaurant to a row of smelly dustbins. "Help yourself to the best grub in town," he said and immediately jumped up against the first bin and knocked the lid off.

Benny jumped up too but the bin was taller than he thought. He managed to nudge the lid off but no matter how much he stretched and strained he couldn't reach the food.

"Hey!" he yelped. "This isn't fair."

"Why not?" muttered Harry through a mouthful of carrots and trifle.

"I can't reach," yelled Benny. "I haven't got long legs like you."

"Well, jump in!" snapped Harry impatiently.

"Jump in!" spluttered Benny. "How will I ever get out again?"

"Really, you're a dope at times," scoffed Harry.

"You can get out exactly the same way as you got in!"

Benny watched him gobble up a sausage roll covered in cream. "I've no choice," he growled. He took a deep breath and jumped right into the bin.

"Ooh!" he thought.

"It's dark, it's stale,
  it's all very smelly.
  There are cakes, there are buns,
  there's an old squashed jelly.
  There are pies, there are puds,
  there are even roast spuds!
  I can munch and crunch,
  I can chomp and chew.
  I can do what I fancy,
  what I like to do.
  There's no one to hurry me,
  no one to worry me –
  I'll be happy in here for an hour or two!"

But Benny was wrong!

  Suddenly a loud, angry voice bellowed, "Here you – get out of it!"

  Benny stayed perfectly still and listened.

  There was a scuffle of footsteps then Harry gave a loud yelp.

"What's going on?" gasped Benny, quickly poking his head out of the bin. He saw the restaurant owner throw a stone after Harry who was running away across the Common.

"Blooming, thieving dogs!" he bawled as he banged the lid down on Harry's bin.

"Oh no. He'll kill me!" flapped Benny and he started to burrow down to the bottom of the bin. Greasy chips, cold gravy and mushy peas trickled over his head and back.

"UGH!" groaned Benny as a stale apple pie got stuck in his ear. "You can have too much of a good thing."

But at least the restaurant owner didn't see him! He slammed the lid down on Benny's bin, making his ears ring with the clatter, then he stormed off. "Thank goodness he's gone," sighed Benny and tried to scramble free, but coming up was much harder than going down! It was so dark he could hardly tell the top from the bottom and every time he moved, he slipped and skidded on some greasy slime. He finally wriggled out and started to push hard against the lid. It wouldn't move. He frantically scratched at it with his claws, it still wouldn't move. In desperation he rocked the bin from side to side, he felt sick and dizzy as it crashed backwards and forwards sending soup and gravy splashing all over his body.

"I've got to get out!" whined Benny, but he was too frightened to bark and too scared to cry. Suddenly he heard a low, gruff voice.

"Are you all right in there?"

It was Harry!

"No, I'm not all right!" yapped Benny. "Get me out, oh, please get me out!"

"Hang on," snapped Harry and he tried to tip the lid off. It wouldn't budge. "It's jammed," he whispered. "I can't shift it on my own. I'll have to fetch Charlotte."

"Oh dear," whimpered Benny, as he started to slip down into the slime once more. "Bring anybody you want, but do it quickly, before I suffocate in here."

"Right," panted Harry. "I'll be as quick as I can."

Benny heard him rush off and waited, and waited, sinking deeper and deeper into the smelly, sloppy mess.

"Oh, please come soon," he moaned, and something did come, but it wasn't Harry.

It was a loud, churning, grinding, cranking, clanking machine! Benny heard the noise and started to tremble.

"Whatever can it be?" he thought.

Suddenly he felt himself being lifted high into the air. His stomach turned right over as he was bounced along.

"Who's carrying me, where am I going?" he whined.

Little did he know he was heading straight for the refuse lorry! The dustbinman dumped the bin onto the ground,

whipped the lid off and was just about to whizz the rubbish, and Benny, into the grinding machine.

"NO!" gulped Benny, still buried under the food.

"DON'T DO IT!" screamed the children as they tore across the Common with Harry at their side.

"Don't do what?" said the dustbinman.

"Don't flatten me!" howled Benny as he finally came up for air. The dustbinman was speechless.

"What the heck's going on?" he spluttered.

"That's our dog," yelled Bella and Jack as they rushed up and grabbed hold of Benny.

"Thank heavens you're here," he whimpered. "Please get me out."

But he was stuck tight. The four of them grabbed hold of him, counted to three then gave a mighty yank – SQUELCH! Out he came! But what a sight he was. He was covered from the tip of his tail to the points of his ears with rotten, smelly, slimy food!

"Ugh!" said Bella.

"Yuk!" said Jack.

"Yum!" slobbered Harry and licked all the good bits off.

"I've had enough of this!" barked Benny and jumped right into the river – SPLASH! It was lovely. He swam round and round until he was clean again, then he jumped out and shook himself all over Harry.

"Serves you right!" he growled.

"Come on," said Bella. "Let's take you home."

"Yes," said Jack. "It's time for tea."

"Oh no!" groaned Benny. "I never want to eat again."

But, of course, he did, the very next day. Only this time he made sure it wasn't out of the dustbins!

# Joke Time

When is a brown dog not a brown dog?
When it's a greyhound.

Did you hear about the sheep dog trials?
Three of the dogs were guilty.

What goes "Wuff-wuff, tick-tick?"
A watchdog.

What would you do if you found
a Great Dane asleep in your bed?
Sleep somewhere else!

Dog to dinosaur's skeleton,
"I've a bone to pick with you!"

"Doctor, Doctor, our dog keeps thinking he's a hen."
"How long has he been like this?"
"About a month."
"Why didn't you bring him earlier?"
"Sorry, we needed the eggs!"

"Doctor, Doctor, I keep thinking I'm a dog."
"Lie down on the couch and I'll examine you."
"I can't, I'm not allowed on the furniture."

A man went into a pet shop and said,
"Do you have any dogs going cheap?"
"No, Sir," said the shop-keeper. "All ours go bow-wow."

Why is it that every time the door
bell rings, my dog goes into a corner?
He's a boxer.

Willie: "It's raining cats and dogs outside."
Bob: "I know, I've just stepped into a poodle."

"I've lost my dog."
"Why don't you put an advertisement in the paper?"
"Don't be silly, he can't read."

First Clever Dick: "Every day my dog and I go for
a tramp in the woods."
Second Clever Dick: "Does the dog enjoy it?"
First Clever Dick: "Yes, but the tramp's getting a bit
fed up."

WHAT DO YOU GET IF YOU CROSS A DOG WITH A JEEP?

A LANDROVER!

# Caring for your dog

Harry quickly outgrew his cardboard box-bed and Charlotte wanted to buy him a basket of his own. Her Mum and Dad suggested she should wait until Harry had finished teething, that's around six months, so that he wouldn't bite his new basket to pieces. Puppies will chew their way through anything at this stage, so don't leave your best slippers lying around or they'll be in shreds when you next see them!

Harry didn't like his dog collar to start with. It annoyed him and the identity disc rattled in his ear, but Charlotte put it on him for a few hours every day and he gradually got used to it.

When Charlotte got her new puppy home, the first thing she wanted to do was take him out for a walk, but her parents said she couldn't. A young pup can't go out on the streets, or mix with other dogs, until he's been vaccinated. Charlotte was very disappointed but she didn't want to put Harry in danger, so she settled for exercising him in the garden and occasionally put a lead on him so he would become familiar with it.

Harry was given his own food and water bowl and had four meals a day to start with. At first, he had two milky meals and two meat meals. Charlotte gradually dropped one of the milky meals and then the other. Now he's on one meal a day and that's usually enough for an average-size dog.

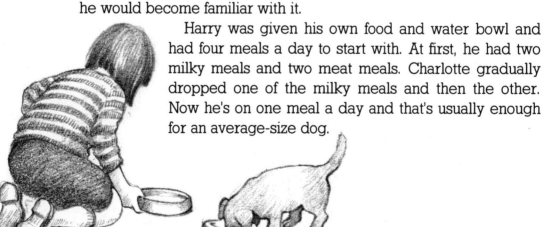

\*  How can you stop your dog from
   barking in the back garden?
   Put him in the front garden.

Harry has very regular meal times and he's never fed from the table by any of the family. When he was a puppy, he was always put outside after meals and Charlotte praised him to the sky if he made a mess in the garden and not in the house!

When Harry was naughty, Charlotte was very clear in showing her disapproval. She didn't nag and scold him, making him confused and anxious, she just took hold of him by the scruff of the neck and said "NO!" very firmly.

Harry, like any other pup, quickly responded to praise, he was eager to learn and keen to please. Charlotte taught him through patience and love and, when he was older, she took him along to the local dog-training classes where he was taught the basic commands like 'heel', 'sit', 'come' and 'stay'. A pup, like a baby, has a lot to learn. The world is opening up for him and it can be both exciting and frightening. Be patient with him, and gentle too. Let him have quiet times when he can sleep and play. Don't always be waking him up and shouting in his ears, and don't drag him around the house as if he were a soft toy! Remember, he's real. Give him time to grow up into a strong, healthy dog who will be your friend for life.

# Benny lends a hand

$O$ne hot summer day Benny lay sprawled out on the lawn and watched Mr Moss digging down at the bottom of the garden.

"He's a bit slow," thought Benny. "I'll pop down there and help him out."

He scampered down to Mr Moss and started to scratch and scrape at the earth with his front paws. It flew up in a shower and scattered in all directions.

"Goodness me, Benny!" said Mr Moss flicking earth off his nose and head and shoulders. "You're not a tidy worker but you're certainly a fast one!"

Benny barked proudly and carried on, but before long he was puffing and panting, and boiling hot too. "COO! This gardening business is harder than it looks," he spluttered.

Little did he know what lay ahead of him!

While Benny finished digging the hole, Mr Moss set up long rows of canes for his beans and peas to grow around.

Benny's big, wagging tail accidently flicked up and down against the canes and in seconds he'd brought the lot clattering down around his ears.

"Ooh! Ouch!" he yelped, but Mr Moss was too cross to be bothered with him.

"Get out of my way!" he snapped.

Benny crept into the garden shed and watched Mr Moss

through a grimy window covered in cobwebs.

"This is a mucky old place," thought Benny, pressing his face right up against the glass, determined to see what was going on outside. He never found out!

His front paws slipped on the neatly-stacked plant pots he'd been leaning against.

"Oh no!" he yapped as the pots whizzed and skidded all over the floor.

He tried to put them back in a tidy pile but finished up making a bigger mess than before! He couldn't stack them, like Dad had done, because he wasn't very good at sorting out the sizes, so he just plonked them all together in a higgledy-piggledy heap.

"I'll get into a load of trouble now," thought Benny – and then he had a brainwave!

"If I dust and tidy this small old shed, Mr Moss will never notice the plant pots."

He started to clean the window with his tongue then decided to dust the shelves with his tail. What he didn't notice was the ball of string starting to unwind. It caught on the end of his tail and went all over the place! In seconds Benny was tied up in knots, unable to move backwards or forwards.

"Oh help!" he howled. "Please come and help me!"

Mr Moss came running to the shed and couldn't believe his eyes.

"Benny!" he shouted. "Can't I leave you alone for five minutes?"

Benny felt very stupid.

"I was only trying to help," he whined, but this time he'd gone too far.

"OUT!" said Mr Moss.

Benny slunk down the path and out of the back gate.

He passed the other gardens and peered in to see what was going on – everybody was out gardening!

There were barrows and rakes,
paper packets of seeds,
long garden hoses,
big piles of weeds.
There were carrots and potatoes,
tomatoes and beans,
Marrows and pumpkins –
the biggest he'd seen!

But there was nobody to play with. Suddenly Benny spotted some pigeons cleaning themselves on a rooftop.

"Hey! Come down here and play with me!" he yapped.

"*Coo . . . Cooo*," went the pigeons.

"Oh, never mind all that silly singing, just come down here and play!" barked Benny, but the pigeons took fright and flew up, circling the sky above his head.

"You're no good to anybody!" snapped Benny and stalked off.

There were some cheerful-looking ducks quacking on the 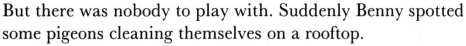 river bank.

"Hey, will you play with me?" yelped Benny as he ran towards them.

"*Whack whack whack*" squawked the ducks as they splashed into the water.

"Oh, don't you start," snapped Benny and slumped under a tree, fed up and bored.

A lady passing by stopped to stroke him.

"Cheer up," she said. "I've got just the thing for you."

She reached into her basket and brought out a bag of bones.

"I've just been to the butcher's for my dog," she said. "But he can spare one of these bones for you."

She put the biggest of the lot on the ground in front of Benny.

"Thank you," he barked. "I feel better already."

He gobbled both ends but there was still lots of meat left.

"I'll take it home," he thought, "and bury it somewhere really safe."

He slipped back into the garden and looked about for the hole he'd been digging that morning. Mr Moss had filled it in and it had funny green plants dotted on the top of it.

"I'll soon get rid of that lot," thought Benny.

In no time at all he'd dug another hole, into which he carefully dropped his precious bone.

"Nobody will ever find it!" thought Benny covering it up and feeling very pleased with himself.

Just then Mr Moss came walking down the path. He also looked very pleased with himself.

"Well, Benny," he said. "What do you think of my lettuce plants?"

Benny looked around, but he couldn't see any plants anywhere.

"What's he talking about?" he thought, and then he realised – he'd just dug them up!

Mr Moss was furious. He made Benny help him collect up the wilting plants and together they put them back again. The only problem was that Benny couldn't tell the tops from the bottoms so he just rammed them into the soil and hoped for the best. When he caught sight of Mr Moss's scowling face he crept away and hid. By tea-time Mr Moss had finished.

"I'll water them now," he said.

"And I'll get out of the way!" thought Benny, but he couldn't even do that properly. His legs got tangled up in the long, trailing loops of the hose pipe lying across the path.

"Will you MOVE!" bawled Mr Moss.

"I would if I could!" snapped Benny, desperately trying to free himself. He finally wriggled out but knocked the nozzle from Mr Moss's hand and sent the water splashing all over the place!

"I've just about had enough of this!" stormed Mr Moss.

"And so have I," snarled Benny.

They both stomped indoors and avoided each other for the rest of the day, but later that evening Benny crept up to Mr Moss as he watched the telly.

"Sorry," he whimpered, pressing his head against Mr Moss's leg.

"I know you mean well," said Dad. "But next time I'm working in the garden why don't you just run out and play on the Common?"

"I will," yapped Benny. "Don't you worry – I will!"

# Benny's Favourite Crossword

## Across
1. The common Benny plays on, ____ even in the winter! (9)
5. When Collie dogs count them, they don't fall asleep. (5)
6. One of the basic commands. (3)
7. Pekinese dogs were worshipped in the Far ____. (4)
10. Some breeds of dog are very expensive, especially the ____ breeds. (4)
11. Benny lived on one of these before he came to the Common. (5)
12. Benny took this from the Christmas tree. (4)
13. The tallest dog is a Great ____ . (4)

## Down
1. A puppy soon learns to recognize its ____ . (6)
2. Stray dogs are cared for in an Animal ____ . (7)
3. Bella and Jack's last name. (4)
4. Terriers are often used to catch these. (4)
8. The parents of a pedigree dog are the same ____ . (5)
9. If you want your dog to obey you, you must ____ it. (5)
11. You *might* get rich if you put a ____ on the winning greyhound. (3)

# Find Benny's bone!

**Start here**

1 2 3 4 5 6 7 8 9 10 11 12 13 14 15 16

34 35 36 37 38 39 40

Mr Moss sees Benny sneaking out, calls him back. Return to beginning.

Benny gets the right smell. Run on three squares.

Benny gets waylaid by a bag of cold chips. Miss a go.

Benny spots a policeman on the beat, remembers he's left his dog collar in the house, hides. Miss a go.

Benny spots some joggers, follows th Go back four squa

Benny gets scared by a big Alsatian, hides. Return to 5.

Benny sees Harry heading for the bone patch. Runs on. Move on five squares.

Bella and Jack are out looking for him. Benny hides in a bush. Miss a go.

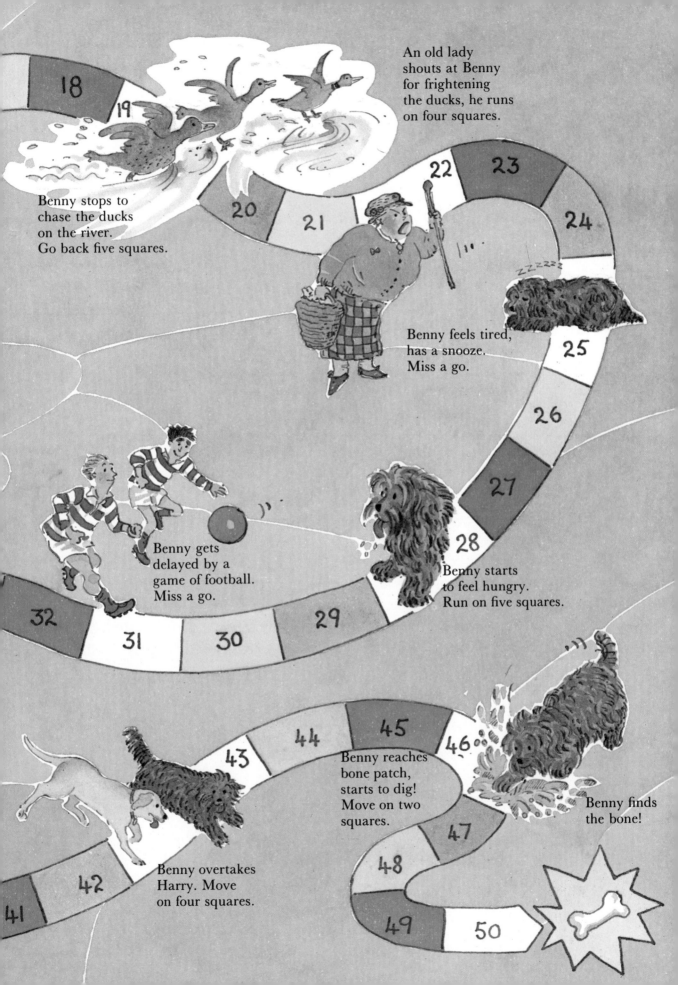

An old lady shouts at Benny for frightening the ducks, he runs on four squares.

Benny stops to chase the ducks on the river. Go back five squares.

Benny feels tired, has a snooze. Miss a go.

Benny gets delayed by a game of football. Miss a go.

Benny starts to feel hungry. Run on five squares.

Benny reaches bone patch, starts to dig! Move on two squares.

Benny finds the bone!

Benny overtakes Harry. Move on four squares.

# Going to the Vet

When Harry first went to see the Vet, it was for a general check-up but the Vet also talked to Charlotte about worming and vaccination. He stressed that Harry was *not* to be allowed out, and not to play or mix with other dogs until he'd completed his course of vaccinations.

Mothers take their new babies to the clinic for a course of injections that will protect them from diseases as they grow up. It's exactly the same thing for a dog-owner and her pup. Puppies need to be vaccinated against distemper, hepatitis, leptospirosis and parvovirus, otherwise they can become very ill and, in some cases, die.

Harry had his first vaccination at about twelve weeks. A month later, Charlotte took him back for his second injection and that was it; his course was completed, and a week later he could run out and play!

The Vet told Charlotte that the vaccinations don't last a life-time. It's very important that she remembers to take Harry back to the surgery every year for a booster injection.

Worming can be a tricky business with young pups. They are born with roundworm and should be wormed early but do let the Vet advise you, and remember, he knows best.

Harry's first months with Charlotte were extremely important. It's in those early months that a puppy gets to know and trust his family, he receives his first training and starts to be interested in the big world outside. It's a vital time in his development because he wants to play and explore, run and bark, tease and chase but, like a baby, he needs to come home to the owner he loves, and settle down in the safety of his own home.

Nowadays, not many dogs have awful lives like poor, old Benny with the bargee but if you should see something cruel happening to any animal then report it to the RSPCA immediately. If you should find a stray dog, don't keep it, notify the police or take it to your local animal shelter. It may belong to somebody who is desperately trying to find it.

Remember, love your dog, train him well and understand him too. Make him, like Benny, the best friend you've ever had!

## Benny gets lost

One day Benny was out on the Common sniffing around the benches and inside the litter bins.

"Not much in here," he thought and set off for town with his tail held high and his eyes bright with excitement. He stopped at his favourite litter bin right outside the town hall, it was cram-full of delicious rubbish.

> There was melted chocolate, a bag of crisps,
> the end of a sausage and some greasy chips.
> There were four stale buns, some peppermint toffee,
> a smelly hot-dog and a pool of spilt coffee!

Benny guzzled and guzzled. He only came up for air when he'd eaten the lot, then he flopped to the ground – too full to move! Little did he know he was being watched . . .

"That poor dog must be a starving stray," thought a kind old lady sitting on a bench opposite.

"I'd better phone the RSPCA and ask them to come and pick him up."

While the lady made the phone call, Benny snoozed in the evening sunshine. He only woke up when the town hall clock chimed seven.

"Goodness me," he yawned. "I'd better get a move on or I'll be late for supper!"

It was at that moment that the man from the RSPCA turned up.

"There's the stray," said the old lady pointing to Benny. "I'm sure he's starving to death!"

"Me . . . starving?" yapped Benny. "I've never been as full in my life!"

But the man from the RSPCA didn't understand, he just grabbed Benny and tied a rope around his neck.

"Hey! Let me go!" howled Benny. "LET ME GO!"

"Calm down," said the warden. "I'm just taking you to the animal shelter until I can find out where you live."

"I live on Midsummer Common, that's where I live," barked Benny. "Just look at my identity disc and you'll see for yourself."

And then he remembered – he hadn't got his collar round his neck! Bella had taken it off the day before to brush him and he'd hidden it under her bed. It had seemed a great joke at the time, but it wasn't at all funny now.

The warden thanked the old lady and set off across the town with Benny struggling and straining all the way. They stopped outside a tall, dark building and Benny sniffed . . . he could smell dogs, lots of them. He could hear them too, their barks and howls echoed through the house. The warden led him down a corridor and out into a big yard at the back.

There were rows and rows of cages, and all of them had dogs locked up inside. They sprang forwards and rattled the bars as the warden passed.

"Ooh, I don't like it here," whimpered Benny and pressed himself close to the warden's legs. There was an empty cage at the bottom of a long row. The warden gently pushed Benny in, then went off to prepare the dogs' supper.

Benny rushed into a dark corner of the cage and curled up tight, shaking with fear. Suddenly a soft, wet tongue licked his nose. Benny jumped and looked at the dog in the cage next to his.

"I'm Sam," said his neighbour. "Who are you?"

"Benny . . . and I don't like it here. I want to go home!"

"Well, you're lucky," said Sam. "I *never* want to go home."

"Why?" asked Benny.

"It was an awful place," answered Sam.

"I was beaten, half-starved, then kicked out one winter's night. If the RSPCA hadn't rescued me, I'd have been dead long ago."

"But I've got the best home in the world," whined Benny.

"Then you should've stayed there, and not gone wandering," snapped Sam. "Never mind, you'll soon get used to it!"

"I'll never get used to it," groaned Benny and he closed his eyes and thought of Bella and Jack.

Little did he know how worried they were. They'd been out searching for him on the cold, empty common.

"BENNY! BENNY!" they yelled, but their voices just faded away into the dark night.

"Don't worry," said Mum, "he'll be back by morning."

But he wasn't!

Mum phoned the police, but they hadn't seen him.

"We'll try the RSPCA," said Mum.

"Why?" asked Bella. "Benny has an identity disc, if somebody finds him they'll see it and bring him home to us."

"No, they won't," said Mum. "They can't! Look what I found under your bed this morning," and she held up Benny's dog collar.

"Oh no!" sobbed Bella. "Now we'll never find him."

"Yes we will," said Mum and she hurried the children through the town to the animal shelter.

The warden took them into the yard and showed them the rows of cages. They were shocked to see so many stray dogs.

"Where do they come from?" asked Jack.

"All over the place," answered the warden. "Some of them are so badly treated by their families they run away from home, others get lost and a few are just dumped on our doorstep. We try to look after them for as long as we can, hoping their owners will turn up and claim them, but most of them don't."

"Well, we're here," said Jack. "And we want our Benny back."

"Good," said the warden. "Let's see if we can find him."

But they couldn't!

Benny was curled up in a dark corner too weak to stand. He hadn't slept, he hadn't eaten, and he didn't care what happened to him. The children had passed his cage but it looked empty. They were just about to leave when Sam

started to bark at the top of his voice.

"Benny's HERE!" he yapped. "Right here, beside me!"

The other dogs joined in, they whined and growled, snapped and howled.

"What's going on?" shouted Mum over the racket.

"I don't know," said the warden. "But something's got into them."

"I'm sure this one's trying to tell us something," said Jack, going up to Sam's cage.

Sam went wild, he threw himself at the bars of Benny's cage and started to scratch at them.

"He's here!" he yelped. "Right here!"

Bella peered in and suddenly spotted Benny in the dark corner.

"I can see him!" she yelled. "BENNY! BENNY! We're here!"

Benny looked up and blinked.

"Am I dreaming?" he thought.

When the cage door flew open and the children rushed in, he knew he wasn't dreaming! With a bound he was in their

arms, snuggled up tight and covered in kisses.

"Come on," said Mum. "Let's take this lost boy home."

"Yes! Yes!" yapped Benny. "Take me back to where I belong."

Then he remembered Sam and the other dogs.

"Goodbye," he barked. "And thank you for helping me!"

"Goodbye!" they yelped, sad to see him go, but happy for him to have a home of his own.

Benny was overjoyed! As soon as he got back, he rushed upstairs and scrambled under Bella's bed.

"Where's my dog-collar?" he yapped.

Mum smiled and took it out of her pocket.

"Is this what you're looking for?" she asked.

Benny barked and stood quietly while she put it on, he felt much better when it was safely fastened round his neck.

"Now keep it there!" said Bella, tickling his ears.

"And don't ever leave us again," said Jack.

"I won't!" barked Benny. "I love you all too much."

And he snuggled up to the children, happy and free, home, once more, on Midsummer Common.

# Did you know?

Some interesting facts

Did you know that the chow was fattened up on rice and titbits and was part of the daily diet in China and Mongolia?

Did you know that the favourite dogs of the Egyptian Pharaohs were killed on the death of their masters and mummified too?

Did you know that one of Queen Victoria's daughters had the hair from her favourite poodle combed and then spun into a silky shawl for her to wear?

Did you know that wolves and foxes are close cousins of the dog and share many similar characteristics in both their temperament and behaviour?

Did you know that the Pekinese was called the 'Lion Dog' and was considered to be sacred by the Chinese Emperors and their people? Pekinese were unknown outside China until the fall of the Empire in the nineteenth century. The smallest Pekinese were known as 'sleeve dogs' because they were carried about in the long, baggy sleeves of the royal courtiers.

Did you know a husky pup is fully weaned at six weeks and enjoys a diet of artificial milk and minced seal meat!

Did you know that Eskimos still use packs of huskies for hunting the polar bear and the musk ox?

Did you know that poodles were once known as water spaniels and were originally used as gun dogs? They were particularly popular for duck shooting as they were considered to be excellent water retrievers. The fancy fashion for clipping the poodle's coat began for very practical reasons. The weight of the water on the thick, uncut hair of the poodle would have dragged the dog below the surface and possibly drowned it.

# Brave dogs

The monks of St Bernard's Hospice in Switzerland kept and bred dogs in the seventeenth century to guide and rescue travellers from snow drifts. Today's St Bernards are bigger and heavier than the original ones, some can weigh up to 21 stone, the weight of two grown men.

In the Second World War more than 10,000 dogs were used to take messages and supplies across enemy lines. They often carried out this duty while a battle was in progress, keeping quiet while shells were exploding all around them. These war dogs could detect a land mine, carry small supplies of ammunition, find wounded soldiers and airmen, and sniff out the presence of an enemy.

Army dogs are tattooed on the left ear so they can be identified.

When the Romans conquered Britain, they were very impressed with the ferocious British mastiffs, which were larger and fiercer than their own. They took many of them back to Rome where they were used in the amphitheatre to fight wild beasts for sport and entertainment.

# Some recorded facts about dogs

**Largest** The St Bernard, the heaviest on record is 21 stone 11 lb (138,34kg)

**Tallest** The Great Dane and the Irish wolfhound, the tallest on record is a Great Dane measuring 40½ inches (102,9cm)

**Smallest** The Yorkshire terrier, the chihuahua and the toy poodle. Miniature versions of all of these breeds have been know to weigh less than 16 oz (453 g) when adult. The smallest on record is a 10 oz (283 g) Yorkshire terrier who was 3½″ tall at shoulder height.

**Oldest** 29 years 5 months (dogs rarely live over 20).

**Largest Litter** A foxhound bitch who gave birth to 23 puppies.

**Most Prolific** A champion greyhound called 'Low Pressure who sired 2,414 puppies between the years 1961–69.

**Top Trainer** Mrs Barbara Woodhouse, the fastest and most successful trainer. She trained 17,136 dogs to obey the basic commands between the years 1951–82.

What do you get when you cross a jelly with a sheep dog?
The collie-wobbles.

# Grooming your dog

You may desperately want a dog of your own but, for one reason or another, this may not be possible. Don't despair, ask a friend or a neighbour if you can walk their dog, or phone up the local animal shelter. They often welcome volunteer help and there should be plenty of exercising and grooming for you to do.

Charlotte trained Harry from a very early age to accept his daily grooming. He didn't need much to start with but as he got older it became an important part of his daily routine.

Harry has a medium-length coat, which is easy to care for but, like all Labradors, he moults rather a lot.

It's important to train your dog to keep off the furniture and the beds. It's neither hygienic nor sensible to have him lounging around all over the house. His place is his basket and he should know this from the earliest age.

Charlotte regularly cleans out Harry's basket. Fleas lay their eggs in warm places, like the bedding in a dog's basket. If this should happen, burn the bedding and thoroughly disinfect the basket, otherwise you'll never control the fleas.

Charlotte likes to groom Harry regularly, not just to make him look clean and beautiful, but also because it is the best way of checking his fur for fleas, ticks and lice. If you should ever spot any of these parasites, take your dog straight to the Vet. The sooner they're treated the better.

Charlotte uses a steel comb and a brush to groom Harry. She works through all his hair and doesn't just skim over the top. When she reaches a tangled clump of hair, she loosens it with her fingertips and doesn't just drag it out. That would hurt Harry. (Charlotte often forgets to do Harry's feet and face. He doesn't mind one bit, but Mum reminds her to finish him off. It's worth it in the end!)

Charlotte only baths Harry when he's dirty or smelly; too much washing can dry out the natural oils in a dog's hair. She uses dog shampoo, which she thoroughly rinses out, then she dries Harry as quickly as she can so he won't catch a chill.

Harry usually makes quite a fuss about bath-times and grooming, but afterwards he's always rather pleased with his pretty, sweet-smelling self!

# In the waiting room

# Benny and the bright star

Christmas was coming, Benny's first on Midsummer Common, and he was wild with excitement.

The weather had turned sharp and frosty, the days were short and night came early. The world was damp, dark and chilly but indoors everything was wonderful.

Coloured streamers decorated every room, holly, flecked with bright berries, gleamed in every corner, and mistletoe dangled in all the doorways. When Dad brought a big pine tree home and stuck it in a tub in the hall, Benny began to think everybody was going silly in the head.

"Trees belong outside!" he yapped.

Bella laughed and cuddled him.

"It's Christmas, Benny, everything's magic at Christmas time."

Five minutes later Benny began to understand what she meant. The tall, thin pine tree had been transformed into a shimmering tower of coloured light. Tinsel flickered on its branches and fairy lights twinkled all around it. But it was the big, silver star tied to the top that caught Benny's eye. It was the loveliest thing on the tree and every night he would sit and stare at it glittering brightly in the dark hall. As Christmas drew nearer, the children stopped playing their indoor games and started to rehearse for the pantomime. It was to be held in the school hall on the evening of the last day of term.

Mum was busy making costumes. Jack was a donkey and Bella had the lead part, she was the bright star, and she led

everybody in the play to the secret palace of the little prince. Benny desperately wanted to join in, but there didn't seem to be a part for him.

"Never mind," he thought. "At least I'll get to see the show."

But that didn't happen either. Everybody got dressed up on the big night but when it came to leaving, nobody thought about Benny.

"Hey, you lot!" he snapped. "I'm coming too."

"Can't we smuggle him in?" asked Jack.

"Certainly not!" said Mum. "Now come along, or we'll be late."

"Mean old things!" howled Benny after them, but he was determined to go!

He ran around the house looking for a window or a door that had been left open. He finally found the dining room window slightly ajar.

"This'll do," thought Benny.

He wriggled out and scampered quickly across the Common and into town. He was careful to stay behind the crowds of people heading towards the school, he didn't want to be caught by Dad and sent back home. When he got to the school hall he was just about to walk in when the head master grabbed him by the collar.

"Sorry," he said. "No dogs allowed."

"Grown-ups are spoilsports!" growled Benny as he sneaked round the corner and waited for the next group of people to pass. When they were on a level with him, he

scuttled into the middle of them and slipped into the hall unnoticed. Once inside, he slipped behind the long curtains and stayed perfectly still. Suddenly the lights went down, the orchestra struck up and the show started! Benny poked his head around the curtain and watched it all. There was lots of singing and dancing to start with then Jack the donkey came on with some other children dressed up as animals. Bella flitted in wearing a pretty silver leotard but there was something terribly wrong with her. Her face was red and swollen, her eyes were full of tears and every time she spoke her chin wobbled.

"What's the matter with her?" thought Benny anxiously.

When the interval came, he slipped back behind the curtain but peeped out occasionally to see what was going on. Suddenly he spotted Bella rushing up the aisle and throwing herself into Mum's arms.

Benny couldn't stand it one minute longer. He ran straight to Dad's side and barked, "What's going on?"

Dad was too concerned with Bella to worry about Benny.

"What is it, love?" he gently asked.

"I can't do it if I can't find the star," sobbed Bella.

"But you had it," said Mum. "Where did you put it?"

"Oh, I don't know," cried Bella. "I can't find it anywhere!"

"We've got to do something," said Mum, nearly in tears herself.

It was at that moment that Benny had one of his brainwaves.

"I'll get you a star!" he yelped and before anybody could stop him, he'd belted out of the hall and was half-way down the street. He tore through the town and across the Common, he was gasping for breath but he never stopped once. He squeezed in through the window and ran straight to the Christmas tree.

"That's what I want!" he panted as he stared up at the far-away star shimmering in the dark hall. "But how on earth will I get it down?"

He couldn't just knock the tree down, but neither could he climb it and it was too high to jump up.

"I've got to get it!" growled Benny. Staring up, he suddenly realised that the tip-top branch of the Christmas tree almost touched the landing above.

He bounded up the stairs and shoved his head through the bannisters, the tree was much closer from there. He pushed his paw through and stretched it towards the star, but no matter how much he tried he simply couldn't reach it.

"I'll try the other end!" thought Benny and he turned about and shoved his bottom through the gap. It was much

harder to keep his balance but if he wagged his tail up and down, and round and round, he could feel it flicking against the edges of the star. Suddenly it whizzed off the tree and fell, flashing, to the ground.

He ran down the stairs and gently picked it up in his mouth.

"This should make Bella smile again," thought Benny as he set off through the town towards the school. This time nobody stopped him at the school door. He scampered down the aisle and dropped the star at Bella's feet.

"Oh Benny, I love you!" cried Bella, grabbing the star and hugging him at the same time. Then she rushed off to change.

Mum asked the headmaster if Benny could watch the second act. He agreed and Benny sat quietly on Dad's knee. This time Bella was radiant. Her face glowed with pleasure and whenever she moved, the star glittered in the soft lights.

When the play finished the curtain dropped and everybody started to clap and cheer. Benny couldn't keep quiet for a second longer.

"Well done, Bella!" he howled. "Well done, Jack!"

The curtain rose and all the children bowed to the audience. The headmaster stepped onto the stage and thanked them all for a wonderful performance, then he added, "But there's somebody else I'd like to congratulate. Ladies and Gentlemen, would you please show your appreciation for Benny – the star of the show!"

Benny went all wobbly! He had never felt so shy in the whole of his life.

"I can't go up there!" he whimpered, but Mum thought differently. She proudly marched him onto the stage and Bella and Jack lifted him onto their shoulders. The audience clapped and cheered so loudly Benny thought the roof might lift off!

He saw the crowds,
blinked at the lights.
They cried "Bravo!"
"You've saved the night!"
Benny shrugged, and cringed, and blushed –
"Goodness gracious, what a fuss!"

# Goodbye, Benny!

Benny! Benny! Come out and play,

down on the Common and stay all day.

*Come on,    Benny,    it's    time to go,*

*but we'll be back    if    you say so.*

Now we know
just what to do,
if we have a dog
as nice as you.

*Chorus*

We'll bath and brush
and fuss and feed,
and do the things
that puppies need.

*Chorus*

We're leaving now
but we'll be back,
on Midsummer Common
with Bella and Jack

*Chorus*